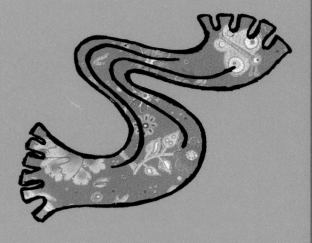

What does Grandma get?

What does Ian get?

What does Ian's baby sister get?

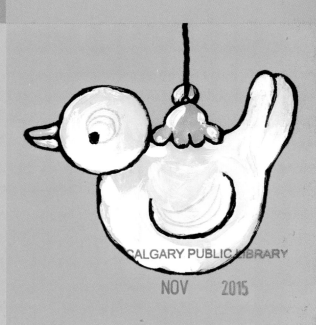

First published in Belgium and Holland by Clavis Uitgeverij, Hasselt – Amsterdam, 2011
Copyright © 2011, Clavis Uitgeverij

English translation from the Dutch by Clavis Publishing Inc. New York
Copyright © 2015 for the English language edition: Clavis Publishing Inc. New York

Visit us on the web at www.clavisbooks.com

Ian Celebrates Christmas written and illustrated by Pauline Oud
Original title: *Kas viert Kerstmis*
Translated from the Dutch by Clavis Publishing

ISBN 978-1-60537-234-1

This book was printed in August 2015 at Proost Industries NV,
Everdongenlaan 23, 2300 Turnhout, Belgium

First Edition
10 9 8 7 6 5 4 3 2 1

Ian
Celebrates Christmas

Pauline Oud

Clavis
NEW YORK

It's almost Christmas. Ian and Dad
have bought a beautiful pine tree.
The tree is very heavy.

Carefully, they shuffle
through the snow.
Oops, sometimes they
slide a bit.
"Thanks for helping, Ian!"
Dad says. "What a strong boy
you are!" Ian and Dad bring
the Christmas tree home as fast
as they can.

The tree is really big. It just barely fits in the living room.
"Let's decorate the Christmas tree," Mom says,
and she begins by hanging lights on the tree.

Ian takes Christmas garlands out of the box.
He also sees beautiful, shining ornaments.
"Look," Ian says to Flap, "a golden globe with dots,
and a cute silver bird."

"Be careful with the globes.
They break easily," Mom says.
Ian takes a big globe
out of the box. He is very
careful, but... CRASH!
The globe falls to the ground.
"Oops, broken!" Ian says.
He had a bit of a fright.
The beautiful globe has
smashed into hundreds
of little pieces.
"Don't worry, Ian,"
Mom says.
"I've got an idea.
Come along."

Mom and Ian make pretty decorations
to hang on the Christmas tree.
Mom cuts stars and angels
out of paper. Ian decorates them
with colored pencils and glitter
paint. "This Christmas star will
shine!" Ian tells Flap cheerfully.
"Look," Mom says. "I'll attach
ribbons and then you can hang
all your decorations on the tree."

Once Ian has put on his pajamas,
he looks at the Christmas tree.
"Look, Flap, I made this star!"
"Come on, Ian," Dad calls,
"you have to go to bed now.
Tomorrow is a very
special day."

"Yes," Ian answers.
"Tomorrow is Christmas!"

Before he goes to bed, Ian wants to see his sister.
"Quietly now," Dad whispers. On tiptoe they walk
to the cradle. Ian hangs a star above the cradle.
"You're so sweet," Dad whispers. "Did you make
that yourself?" "Yes," Ian answers quietly.
"For my baby sister."

The next day Ian wakes up very early.
He puts on his fanciest clothes. "Wow!"
Ian yells when he gets downstairs.
"Presents!" "Yes," Mom laughs.
"It's Christmas! Maybe you'll get
a present this evening."

BRRRINNNGG! Someone has rung the bell.
Ian runs to the door. "Granddad! Grandma!"
he shouts happily. Grandma gives Ian a big
kiss and Granddad lifts him high in the air.
"Merry Christmas," they say.
"You're looking very
handsome today."
"Yes," Ian answers.
"It's Christmas!"

"Granddad, come and look!" Ian calls.
"Wow, what a beautiful Christmas tree," Granddad says.
"But something is missing." Ian looks at the tree carefully.
Underneath there are presents, in the middle there are lights,
garlands, and stars, and on top is a tree topper.
What could Mom and Ian have forgotten?

Granddad puts
a big box on the floor.
"Look," he says.
"This is a crèche.
These are Mary and
Joseph. A very
long time ago
they were
traveling.

Mary was carrying a baby in her belly and she knew
it would be born soon. Because they couldn't find a place
to sleep, they went into a stable where there were an ox
and a donkey. It was nice and warm inside.
    That night baby Jesus was born. There was no cradle
    and baby Jesus slept in a little manger lined with straw."
    Ian and Granddad arrange the figures under the tree.

"Look, little sheep," Ian says as he takes the animals out of the box. "Yes," Granddad continues his story. "There were some shepherds watching their sheep close to the stable. Suddenly they saw an angel. 'Do you see that big star?' the angel asked the shepherds. 'Follow the star and you will see a stable where a very special baby has been born. His name is Jesus and he will make everyone happy.' There were three kings who also saw the star. They brought gifts for the little baby," Granddad says. "That's why we celebrate Christmas today. It's baby Jesus' birthday.

And that's why you might get a present too, later this evening."
"Ian! Granddad!" Dad calls from the kitchen. "It's time to eat! Come to the table."

"Goody!" Ian says when
he sits down at the table.
"Everything looks so pretty,"
Grandma says.
"What a feast!" Granddad agrees.
Dad puts out almost all the lights.
The candles glow.
"Wow!" everyone says.

"Enjoy your meal,"
Mom says.
"Yummm!" Ian cheers.
He has already given
Flap a slice of bread.

After dinner Ian gives Grandma
a present. It's a lovely scarf.
Baby sister gets a colorful rattle.
Then it's Ian's turn. He opens a present.
"What is it?" Granddad asks.
"It's probably shaving cream!"
"No!" Ian laughs.
"A beautiful bouquet of flowers?"
Granddad guesses.
"No, it's something else,"
Ian says happily.
"Wow! Look what I got,
Granddad!"

Later, when Ian is in bed,
Mom reads him his new book.
Ian has chosen one of the sheep from the crèche
to sleep with him. It's lying on his pillow.
"Good night, sweet dreams," Mom says.
Ian yawns. "Christmas is great," he whispers
to Flap and the sheep. "See you tomorrow!"
Then Ian falls fast asleep.

**What you need to make
a Christmas star:**
   colored construction paper
   ribbon
   hole punch
   colored pencils or crayons
   glue

How to make a Christmas star:
   Trace this star onto the paper or
   draw your own. Cut out the star
   and decorate it. Make a hole in the
   star with the hole punch, and attach
   the ribbon. Your Christmas star is
   ready!